© KVACK!
The Frog Prince
Text: Ulf Stark
Illustrations/layout: Silke Leffler
Translation: Comactiva Language Partner AB, Sweden
Typesetting: Gyllene Snittet AB, Sweden
Project manager: Lena Allblom, IKEA of Sweden AB
Project coordinator: Anders Truedsson, TITEL Books AB
Produced by IKEA of Sweden AB
Paper: Arcoset
Printing: Litopat S.p.A., Italy 2014
TITEL Books AB for IKEA of Sweden AB. All rights reserved.

We aim to provide as much inspiration as possible, but with minimal impact on the environment. All our books take the environment into account in every stage of production, from the choice of paper to how we distribute our printed material.

The book you are holding is printed on paper that meets all the requirements for responsible forestry. This means, for example, that the paper raw material comes from trees that are certified to originate from a sustainably managed forest. We print using vegetable-based printing inks without solvents, and the printers are located close to our large markets to avoid long-distance transport to you.

We are also working to develop the printed medium so that it minimises impact on the environment in the future.
Read more about our environmental work at www.ikea.com

ULF STARK

SILKE LEFFLER

The Frog Prince

Princess Klara was bored.

"I've got nothing to do," she moaned.

"Read a story," suggested the queen.

"Sort your stamp collection out," said the king.

"No. I want somebody to play with, somebody my own age," said the princess.

"Well you're a very lucky girl then," laughed the king. "Prince Karl is coming on Thursday. His mummy and daddy are going away."

On Thursday, it was raining. That was a good thing, because
Klara and Karl could jump in puddles. Then they climbed the pear
tree in the castle gardens and each ate a lovely juicy pear.

"I'm glad you came to stay," said Klara.

"So am I," said Karl. "At home I'm hardly allowed to do anything.
Mummy and daddy worry all the time. They think something terrible
will happen to me if I get too happy."

"Why would they think that?"

"Because a fairy said so when I was little," Karl answered. "When I
was born, my daddy invited the fairies of the forest to a party. The first
fairy gave me my singing voice. The second one made me able to wiggle
my ears. But when the third fairy was about to leave her gift, daddy
laughed and whispered: Oh no, that one looks like a right frog. She
wasn't supposed to hear it, but unfortunately she did."

"Was she upset?"

"Of course, she got really angry and said we had better watch out, for
just when we are at our happiest, misfortune will strike!"

"Oh, that's horrible!"

"Nah, it's just one of those things people say when they're angry. As
you can see, nothing has happened. Let's play something else," said Karl.

Princess Klara and Prince Karl played every day. They played bowling with the king's golden apple; they made funny faces in the castle mirrors and swung from the big crystal chandeliers. When they got too hot, the prince simply flapped his ears to fan them. They laughed ever such a lot.

But then the king came along and put his finger to his lips.

"Calm down a bit," he said. "Karl's mummy and daddy said that you can have fun, but not *too* much fun. And what you're doing definitely sounds like *too* much fun to me."

"Let's go outside instead," said Klara.

"Good idea," said the queen. "You can go for a nice quiet walk."

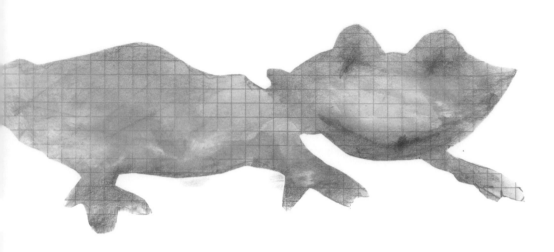

But Karl and Klara did not go for a walk. They lay down in the grass and looked at the clouds instead.

"What's the point of living if you can't play?" asked Klara.

"What's the point of playing if you can't have fun?" said Karl. "Do you want to hear a song?"

Klara certainly did, because no one could sing like Karl. When he sang, all the animals of the forest stopped and listened. The squirrel wiped away a tear with its tail. The owl tilted its head to one side. And the rabbit wiggled its ears in time with the rhythm.

Everybody was happy, and nobody noticed the black cloud creeping over them up in the sky.

"Aha, Prince Karl, so this is where you are," sighed the cloud. "And you certainly look very happy. Remember what I said, misfortune will soon be with you."

But the children didn't hear that.

The next day, Klara and Karl were playing hide and seek.

"Your turn to seek," shouted Karl, and he ran off while Klara closed her eyes and counted to a hundred.

"Too-wit too-woo!" hooted the owl as Karl rushed by. "Be careful. Remember this is the Fairy-Tale Forest."

But the prince's mind was on other things. He got down and hid behind a mossy rock.

What a good hiding-place, he thought.

He sat there giggling, imagining how long it would take Klara to find him, and when she finally did find him behind the rock, she would shout: Oh, there you are! And they would dance around with happiness because they were together again.

"I don't think I could ever be happier than I am right now," Prince Karl said to himself.

But just as he was saying those words, the dark cloud came down into the forest and wrapped him up in a big damp fog.

"Ha ha haaaa," came a husky, murmuring laugh.

"Klara!" the prince tried to shout.

But all that came out was a QUACK!

Klara looked for the prince all day.

"This isn't fun at all!" she shouted. "Come out now!"

But Prince Karl was gone. And even though the king sent out his best scouts and his best tracking dogs, they could not find a single trace of the missing prince.

"Oh, such a misfortune! What will his parents say? You weren't having too much fun, were you?" groaned the king.

"Yes, we were," said Klara. "BUT YOU HAVE TO BE ABLE TO HAVE FUN!"

And she disappeared off to her room and cried and cried, because she was angry and missed her friend.

After a while, she felt a warm little nose on her cheek. It was a mouse with a red woolly hat.

"Don't cry," said the mouse. "We will go and find your friend tomorrow. I have been in lots of fairy tales, so I will help you. As long as I can have a piece of cheese."

The next day, Klara and the mouse set off into the Fairy-Tale Forest.
The first person they met was a little girl with a red riding hood.

"Hello," said the mouse. "Are you off to your grandmother's house
with some biscuits?"

"Yes I am," said the girl. "And I am in a bit of a hurry because I have
to meet a wolf on the way. Is there something I can help you with?"

"I'm looking for Prince Karl," said Klara. "Have you seen him? Or
heard him? He has a lovely singing voice."

"Singing voice, you say? I think you should ask the Musicians."

Before the little girl rushed off, she gave Klara a biscuit from her basket.

"This biscuit is called a 'dream'," said the little girl. "I hope it will be
a nice dream."

The Musicians lived in a house made of sweets and biscuits.

When the mouse and the princess came along, they were busy playing. The donkey was braying, the cat was meowing, the dog was barking and the cockerel was crowing his heart out.

"Do you call that music?" asked the princess once they had stopped.

"Well," smiled the donkey. "We know it sounds terrible. But it is fun. And fun is, after all, what's most important. What can we do for you?"

"We are looking for Prince Karl. I cannot be happy without him," replied Klara.

"Ca-ca-can it be true?" crowed the cockerel.

"Woof-woof-would you believe it? She has done it again," said the dog.

"What? Who?" wondered the princess.

"The wicked fairy," meowed the cat. "Just yesterday she was flying over our house in the shape of a cloud. She told us to stop playing otherwise she'd turn us into something else, just like she had done with a certain giggling prince."

"So it is her," said the mouse. "Where is she?"

"I haven't a clue," said the donkey. "But ask the hare and the hedgehog, they are sure to know, the way they run around. You can ride on me if you like."

The hare and the hedgehog were resting amongst the oak trees. They had been racing.

"What can we do for you?" asked the hare. "Would you like to have a race?"

"No," said Klara. "We're looking for the wicked fairy. Do you know where she lives?"

"When I was out running I heard someone snoring in the cave by the pond. And no one snores quite as horribly as the wicked fairy, it must have been her," said the hare.

"But how will you ever be brave enough to go there?" asked the hedgehog in a scared voice. "She can turn you into anything she likes."

"Maybe while she's sleeping," said the hare. "She usually takes a nap at around this time. I'll run over and take a look."

And quick as a flash, he was off.

"The wicked fairy talks in her sleep when she dreams," said the hedgehog. "Go and listen and you might hear something interesting."

"She's sleeping like a log!" puffed the hare, who was already back.

Klara and the mouse rode on the donkey. As they got nearer, he was not brave enough to go any further, but Klara and the mouse were. Now they stood inside the cave and looked at the wicked fairy, who was sleeping deeply.

"Gosh, she looks really scary," whispered the princess.

"She certainly does. And she is not saying anything either," squeaked the mouse. "She is just snoring."

So Klara took out the biscuit the little girl with the red riding hood had given her.

"Maybe this will help. It is called a 'dream' after all."

Carefully, the princess pushed the biscuit into the sleeping fairy's mouth.

"Frmmpf," was the sound from the fairy as she breathed the dream in, and straight away she started dreaming.

"Ha ha ha! That silly prince will have to catch flies with his tongue for the rest of his life. He is a frog now, and a frog he will stay!" the fairy chuckled, very pleased with herself.

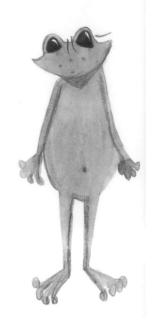

Well, at that Klara got so angry that she tweaked the fairy's nose as hard as she could.

"You rotten wicked fairy you!" the princess shouted. "Make Karl into a boy again!"

The wicked fairy suddenly opened her yellow eyes.

"Never," she sneered. "The only thing that can break the spell is if somebody recognises him. But how could that possibly ever happen? There are thousands of frogs. And you are only allowed one try!"

The moon was shining over the lily pond. This was where the frogs gathered every evening, eating flies and mosquitoes and croaking as frogs do.

"So, where is your little friend then?" teased the fairy.

Klara looked at many different frogs, but they all looked the same. She stopped at one who was smiling and staring at her with big friendly eyes.

"Is that…," she began.

She was just about to say Karl when she heard a croak that sounded different to all the others. It was such a beautiful croak that it made Klara's heart jump, just like a little frog inside her.

There, on a stone a little way off, a frog sat singing so beautifully that the dragonflies were still and the mosquitoes stopped buzzing.

The princess rushed up to the frog, bent down and gave it a kiss.

"Karl!" she cried out happily.

And all of a sudden, the wicked fairy turned into a cloud that blew away. And the frog turned into Karl. He lifted her up and danced around and said:

"Thank you Klara. Now at last we can play as much as we like!"

And the mouse threw its hat in the air and shouted:

"HOORAY!"

And from that day on, Klara and Karl lived as happily as they wanted to forever after.

When they got hot, the prince flapped his ears to fan them. And when they got tired of playing he sang, just as beautifully as always.

And every now and then he gave a little croak.

But they just giggled about that.